THE BOY AND THE MOON

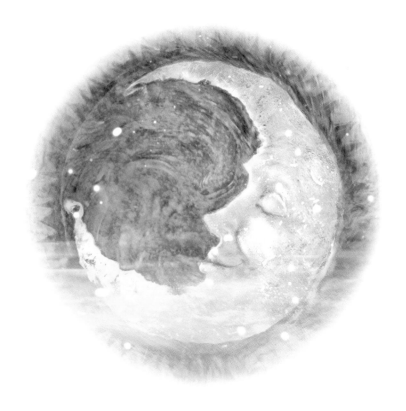

James Christopher Carroll

Published *by* Sleeping Bear Press

It was midnight

when the dancing and the howling began.

They howled at the moon,
they howled at life,
and they howled with all things in the night.

But that night was dusky dark
and the moon got stuck in a tree.

The dancing and the howling stopped, and everyone grew sad.

So they all decided to save the moon.

But owl was afraid of heights,
and rabbit did not feel lucky,
and flower had fainted,
and toad was hiding,
and chicken had a bad, bad bellyache.

So dog tried.

Unfortunately, dogs cannot climb trees.

But children can.

And though he was afraid,
the boy climbed high,
to the very top,
where the moon was crying.

He hugged and he nudged.
He pushed and he pulled.
He jumped, jumped, jumped.

But the moon was still stuck.

Then the boy had a thought,
a delicious thought,
a bright, ripe, red thought.

He picked the apples,
every last one,
and fed them all to the moon,

until the moon was full,
and so big and so round,
she rolled right off the tree

up into the night sky.

And the dancing and the howling began again.

They howled at the moon,
they howled at life,
and they howled with all things in the night.

Good night.

For Elana, Marley, and Oliver
To my mother and father
and Lia

*

Sincere thanks to Anna Olswanger for sharing her wisdom

J.C.C.

Text Copyright © 2010 James Christopher Carroll
Illustration Copyright © 2010 James Christopher Carroll

All rights reserved. No part of this book may be reproduced in any
manner without the express written consent of the publisher,
except in the case of brief excerpts in critical reviews and articles.

Sleeping Bear Press™

315 East Eisenhower Parkway, Suite 200
Ann Arbor, MI 48108
www.sleepingbearpress.com

Sleeping Bear Press is an imprint of Gale, a part of Cengage Learning.

10 9 8 7 6 5 4 3 2 1

Library of Congress Cataloging-in-Publication Data:
Carroll, James Christopher, 1960-
The boy and the moon / James Christopher Carroll.
p. cm.
Summary: A boy and his animal friends go out at night to play,
but when Moon gets stuck in a tree, the boy undertakes a daring rescue.
ISBN 978-1-58536-521-0
[1. Moon--Fiction. 2. Animals--Fiction. 3. Night--Fiction.] I. Title.
PZ7.C2349233Bo 2010
[E]--dc22
2010011856

Printed by China Translation & Printing Services Limited, Guangdong Province, China. 1st printing. 05/2010